I0718194

<u>DANARKO SAGA</u>

Danarko
Ecalain
Carni
Kuriva
Phan'stra

<u>DANARKO NOVELETTES</u>

My Unsung Hero
Shattered Reality

MY UNSUNG HERO

A *Danarko* Novelette

Maxina Storibrook

Silver Grove Publications, LLC

ISBN-13: 978-1-948869-09-6

MY UNSUNG HERO
Author: Maxina Storibrook
Publisher: Silver Grove Publications, LLC
www.maxinastoribrook.com

Paragraph break uses Bergamot Ornaments from dafont.com.

This author is part of the Silver Grove Publications (SGP) family. If you have any questions or wish to browse our other SGP authors, please visit our website for books, products, and submission guidelines. You can also contact SGP for bulk discounts for libraries, stores, and more.

www.silvergrovepublications.com

DEDICATION

In loving memory of those who have suffered from a terminal illness or died for our country. May your memories live on inside your loved ones to be told once again.

AUTHOR'S NOTE

My Unsung Hero was originally created for Maxina's patrons on Patreon as a side story of the *Danarko Saga*. However, Maxina wanted to honor Kael's story and put it into a book form so more people can read about the heroic acts he performed.

It can be treated as a standalone, but the story is best when read alongside the *Danarko Saga*. If it is read in this manner, please read up to Chapter 10 of *Danarko* before continuing.

This is the story of a hero… A hero who lived for what he believed in the most.

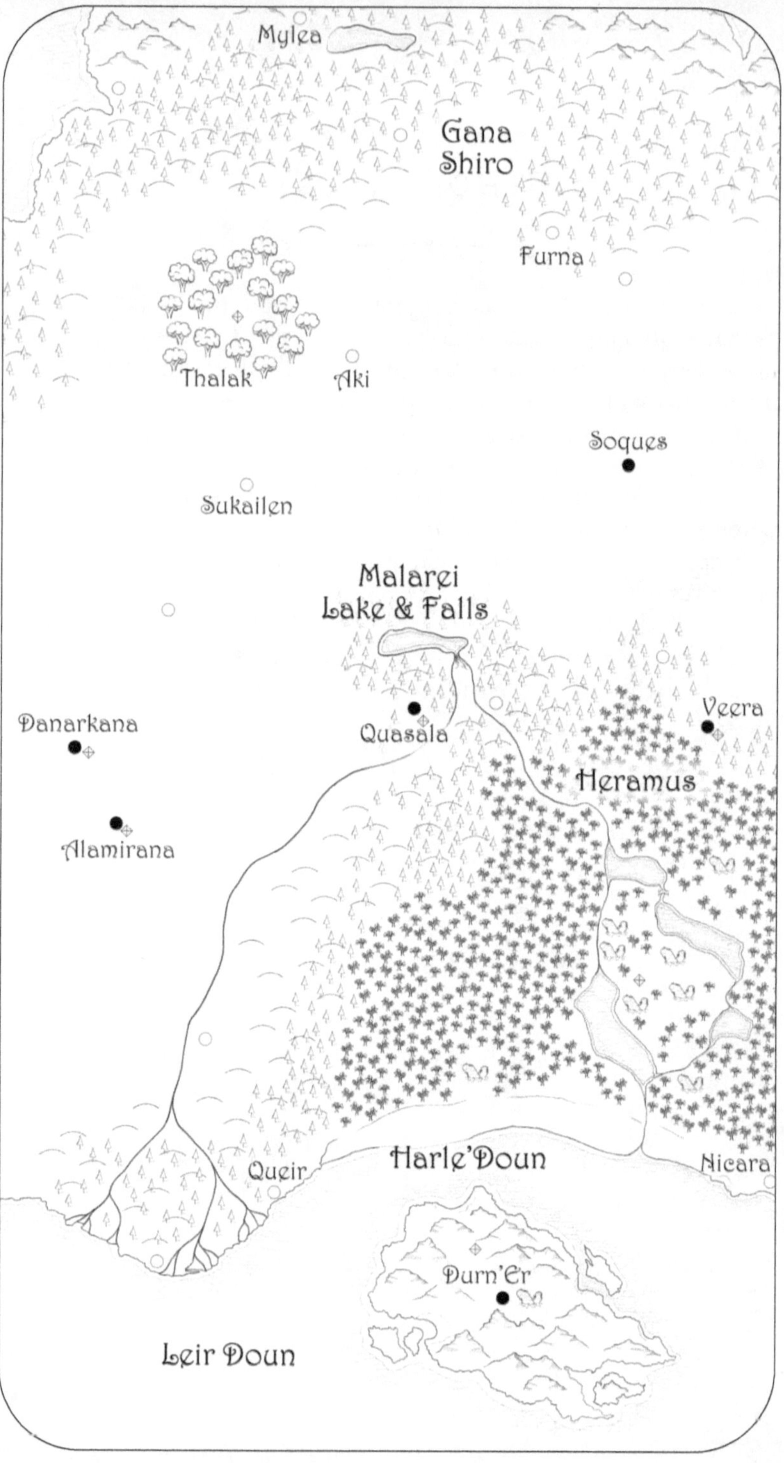

Mylea
Gana Shiro
Furna
Thalak
Aki
Soques
Sukailen
Malarei Lake & Falls
Veera
Danarkana
Quasala
Heramus
Alamirana
Queir
Harle'Doun
Nicara
Durn'Er
Leir Doun

CONTENTS

Prologue

I will never forget the man who had saved me when I was but nine years old. He was so nice and kind to me despite us not being of the same species; he reminded me of the man from my old memories, the ones from long, long ago when I used to be an ambassador.

That man had been a guard sworn to protect the same family I was an ambassador for. He always extended his duties to me, shielding me from the ridicule my kind had received back then.

His story will never be forgotten – neither the guard of forgotten times nor the soldier of the present day. Their unspoken, mighty deeds live on inside me.

This is the story of my hero, Kael Brunet, and how he rescued my family and I from the Heramus.

~ Lyra

Chapter 1
Patrol

Kael strapped on the thick armor as excitement bubbled within him. He had always wanted to be sent to the forest; units who patrolled the border of the cursed forest, the Heramus, always had more exciting stories to share than the simple guards in the city, and he is itching for adventure. He also wanted to see the border for himself, and this gave him the chance.

Raking his hand through his light bronze hair and pushing it back from his pointed elven ears, he exhaled as he mentally checked off the items on his bed and stuffed them into his bag. He was ready, both mentally and physically.

Glimpsing movement out of the corner of his eye, he turned around. His fourteen-year-old sister Kimala stepped into his room, nearly in tears. Her honey blonde hair hung loose and straight around her shoulders, a pretty color that contrasted her blue eyes.

"Please don't go," she begged. Her hands clenched and unclenched the bottom of her shirt.

Kael patted his sister's head. He knew why she was so worried; she lost a friend to the cursed Hemius when she was only nine. It was a thick, poisonous substance that killed an individual from the inside, and the Heramus was named after it. "It's just a patrol," he reassured her. "I'll be back before you know it."

She sniffled, a tear racing down her cheek. "B-but – "

"Hey." He knelt in front of her, taking her hands. "Where's that tincture you've been working on? Surv approved of it, right? I might run across someone who could use it."

She nodded, forcing a smile. "I'll get it for you."

He followed her into the hallway, watching her run to

the end and turn down the next hall. She was training under Medic Surv, Veera's most talented medical advisor, to be a medic. Her biggest goal was to create a tincture that could drastically slow or even stop the spread of Hemius. Many would consider it a lofty dream, but Kael believed in his sister. He had never seen her so dedicated before, so he knew whatever she managed to come up with and that Medic Surv approved of would be worth it.

"Hey, Kael." Codi loped up, his hands shoved deep in his pockets. He shook his black, curly hair out of his moss green eyes. He was the adopted son of Kael's aunt and uncle who had went into hiding over a decade ago to escape the ire of the tyrant of their world; he had shown up, battered and injured, a couple years ago. Kael's parents had taken him in and raised him as their own. "Are you ready for your trip?"

Kael nodded, glancing down the hallway one more time. "Kimala is really upset that I'm leaving, isn't she?" he asked, keeping his voice low.

"Yeah." He shrugged. "But I know you'll make it back. You're the best soldier in Veera!"

"Thanks, kid." Kael grinned and tousled the young boy's hair. "Where's Clarissa?"

"Oh!" He straightened, remembering his original reason for looking for Kael. "Actually, she's waiting for you down in the foyer."

"Thank you." He patted Codi's shoulder. "Keep our ladies safe while I'm gone, all right?"

"Yes, sir!" Codi's fist smacked against his chest as he bowed from the waist – the Alkinian bow of respect.

Kael's gaze softened in affection. "You will be a fine soldier one day, Codi," he murmured, patting his shoulder one more time before walking down the hall.

In the foyer, a pretty redhead chatted with Surana and Jonan, her eyes alit with excitement. Despite being nineteen years old, her rounded ears revealed her Blazhreian heritage. Kael approached, his gaze only on her. She was the most beautiful, precious, and treasured person he had ever known, and he was to marry her in a few months. It felt so surreal, but in the best way possible. He felt as though his heart would explode with how much he cared for her.

Her green eyes turned to meet his blue ones. "Kael!" she exclaimed, her bright smile making the world fall away. He would never grow tired of that smile. "Are you finished packing?"

I want to unpack *now*, he thought, having to swallow down the words before he said them aloud. "I will miss you, love," he murmured instead, giving her a tender kiss on the cheek.

Surana glanced between them, looking like the happiest mother in the world. "Clarissa and I were just talking about wedding venues. I know it is a stretch, but perhaps we could make a special trip to Quasala."

Amused, Kael asked, "Do you want to have the wedding in the capital?"

She nodded excitedly, and her auburn curls bounced around her face. "Oh, it would be so wonderful!"

Kimala dashed out of the hallway, out of breath and face flushed from the run. She handed Kael a small bottle. "I apologize for taking so long. I finally found it."

"Thank you, Kimala," Kael said sincerely, tucking the bottle into a side pouch and winking at his mother's curious gaze. "I will keep it safe."

After a few more minutes of farewells, Kael left the mansion and met up with his partner, Bridget, at the western gate. She was a short woman with brown hair and Blazhreian features; she was Clarissa's best friend and roommate, and she was the one who had introduced Kael and Clarissa to one another. She was laid-back and easygoing most of the time, and she seemed to like the simple job of a Veeran soldier. Within minutes, they were on their way to the edge of the Heramus to patrol and track the progression of the cursed woods.

Trekking through the healthy forest, they were nearing the border when Bridget started some small talk. "I heard you and Clarissa are moving out of the mansion once you're married."

Kael laughed self-consciously, scratching the back of his head. "Y-yeah…"

Bridget gasped, her eyes going wide in mock-disbelief. "It's true, then? You're finally leaving the nest?" Her expression relaxed into a smile. "Seriously, though. I'm happy for you two. You guys are perfect together."

"Thanks, Bridget," he said sincerely.

"But about the wedding," Bridget switched topics, raising an eyebrow.

Kael groaned loudly, finally voicing his opinion. "She wants it in *Quasala*! I thought we were going to have our *honeymoon* in Quasala, not-not the *ceremony*!"

Bridget burst out into loud laughter. "And the truth comes out!" She grinned at her friend. "She really wants to get married in the central field of Cerlail Academy. It's become a new hotspot for weddings and events."

"I respect Uncle Shokain's choice to build it," Kael grumbled discontentedly, "but I never understood the hype. I guess it's because I have no desire to attend."

Kimala did, though; she wanted to be a medic. Even Codi wanted to go after finding out that the the tactical and sorceral wings were starting up different types of combative programs. Both of them had a decent Source rank, a system that registers the strength of the individualized biochemical in one's body, so they would thrive in an academy that would teach them how to utilize it more effectively. On the other hand, Kael had no desire to foster his Source's abilities. He wanted to be able to protect those he loved with his own two hands, not with a power that had corrupted so many historical figures in the past.

"I'm thinking of going." Bridget's quiet confession snapped him out of his thoughts. "They are getting advanced with their team project specialties, such as building structures and designing interiors. I... I want to try it out."

He stared at the armored brunet for a long moment. "You will always have a home in the Veeran troops, no matter what you choose to do."

Her smile strengthened. "Thanks, Kael. Clarissa thought I was crazy when I told her."

Kael shrugged. "I know you like to build." He glimpsed twisted limbs and grey, dead plant life through the trees. "It looks as though we are getting close."

They both went on alert as they drew closer the edge of the Heramus. They stopped on the strange, abrupt line between dead, twisted woods and lush, green forest.

Kael reached into his back pouch and pulled out a rod. He tugged on the sides, extending it to reveal a flexible two-dimensional holographic map on the transparent surface. "This isn't right..."

"What's wrong?" Bridget asked, glancing at the map.

"According to the last Heramus patrol six months ago, we're still thirty tik away from the border."

Bridget glanced at the twisted woods. "It wouldn't have grown that fast, would it?"

"I don't know," he said grimly. "We need to mark how much it has moved, though."

He turned on the track feature on the map, having it mark their progress as they walked the border of the Heramus. Catching movement in his peripheral, he scanned the twisted woods.

"You saw it, too?" Bridget murmured, her gaze sharp.

Kael nodded. "Remain on guard; the Heramus creatures could be hunting."

"They don't normally come this close to the border, though," she argued. "Especially during the day."

"They could have had a starving year." He caught a glimpse of a black substance before it disappeared behind a tree. "Not many people go into the Heramus anymore, after all."

As they continued along the border, a dark form peered at them from behind a gnarly tree and snarled softly.

Chapter 2
Phan

Kael sat on a fallen tree branch, staring gloomily into the Source induced fire. "Cheer up," Bridget encouraged him, heating some meal packs on a metal rack over the fake flames. "At least we haven't run across any Hemius puddles."

"They wouldn't be out this far, anyway," he said, sighing. "I just thought…"

"It would be more exciting?" He looked up to see Bridget smirking at him. "This is what you *want* patrol to be like, Kael. Dead. Boring. Yawn inducing."

He was actually yawning when she said the last part. His jaw snapped shut and he glared at the woman, irritated. "What are you even making? Aren't those just simple field rations?"

She pulled the packs off the heating element, dimming it until a flat disk at the center was visible through the fake yet warm flames. She ripped open one of the packs, a big grin on her face as she exclaimed, "These are Alkinian field rations! I got them from a traveling merchant about a week ago; I thought they would be good to try while on patrol."

"By the flow, how much did you *spend* for this trip?" he muttered, opening his pack. However, as soon as he bit into the bar, a moan slipped by his lips. A delicious, meaty flavor pervaded his senses, tasting just like perfectly seared guldon, an aquatic animal that was a popular delicacy on Alkina.

Bridget guffawed at Kael's reaction, slapping her leg in amusement. "Kael, don't tell me you've never had an Alkinian field ration before!"

"I haven't," he admitted. "Mother may go shopping

with the cooks, but we mainly buy Blazhreian goods. Forget seafood; my sister and father hate it."

Bridget's eyes widened. "Has Clarissa not made her Alkinian-based stew for you yet?"

He tilted his head to the side, curious. Clarissa loved to cook for him, but she hadn't made him any sort of stew. "No. Is it good?"

"Only the *best!*" Bridget exclaimed, throwing her arms out dramatically. "She might be saving it for the first night, honestly. She prides herself in that stew."

"I look forward to eating it, then," he said, smiling.

"Don't tell her you know, though," she warned. "She might have wanted to surprise you with it."

He nodded. "Got it."

They finished their meal and stashed the empty packets inside of a sealed compartment in their bags to hold the trash. Lounging next to the Source fire, they enjoyed the quietness of the forest around them, growing sleepy.

Snap.

It was a quiet yet definitive sound. They stared into the warped woods, eyes straining to see where the sound had come from – or, more specifically, what had *made* the sound. The light from the Source fire only reached so far, though. Naros and Narein were at their darkest time in their cycle around Blazhreia, so not even the twin moons' light could help them.

Kael and Bridget rose to their feet, facing the Heramus. The border was a few yards away; it was a safe distance from them but close enough for monitoring.

"Maybe a branch had fallen," Kael murmured, his voice low.

"Should we at least check it out?" Bridget inquired, fingering the holster containing her multi-function laser gun.

He immediately shook his head. "That's too risky; we can easily be ambushed." He sat down again and faced the border. "I will take the first watch; get some sleep, Bridget."

She nodded, stretching out on the ground and using her pack as a pillow. Kael kept an eye on the Heramus's border, occasionally glancing around to inspect their surroundings.

The next few hours passed in silence. When Kael grew too tired to continue the watch, he woke Bridget and gave her a quick report before falling asleep.

Nothing else happened throughout the night.

The next day, they headed out early to continue their patrol. The woods were quiet – too quiet, in fact. Kael narrowed his eyes, staring through the trees.

"Something is definitely wrong," Bridget whispered.

"Bridget, pull out your gun."

Her gaze snapped to him. "Is it – "

"I don't know." He unholstered his weapon, stepping toward the woods. "I would prefer my hunch to be wrong, though."

Paling, Bridget fumbled with her laser gun, twisting the front barrel clockwise before flipping the safety mechanism up as Kael did the same. The heating mechanisms whirled to life.

Kael creeped forward, his gun up and leading the way. He was hyper-aware of his secondary weapon, his sword, bumping against his armored hip as his eyes flitted about.

"Come out, come out…" he called softly. "We know you're there."

"Kael, behind you!"

He whirled around, automatically training his sights on the huge, black wolf with matted fur and intelligent eyes. Its left forefoot barely touched the ground as it emitted a low snarl ending on a whine.

Recognizing the shapeshifting species, Kael lowered the gun and holstered it before holding out his hand in reassurance. "It's all right," he reassured the giant wolf, slowly approaching it. "We're allies. Are you lost?"

The wolf limped forward to press its cold, wet nose against Kael's hand. "*We were running from some men,*" it said telepathically in an ability called mindspeech as another whimper escaped its muzzle. "*They were trying to capture us. We ran in here, but…*"

Kael knelt in front of the laig'hius, patting the top of its head in sympathy. "We're guards from Veera," he informed the creature. "We patrol the edge of the Heramus to look for survivors and track its progress. You're safe with us."

"I have ointment in my bag," Bridget offered, ruffling in a pouch. "Are you able to change into a bipedal form?"

The wolf dipped its head in affirmation. Limping forward, it laid down on the green earth. Its form stretched and morphed, the fur partially receding to reveal a naked man with an exorbitant amount of chest, leg, and arm hair and lupine ears. His skin was blemished with dark purplish-black bruises along his arms and legs, and an especially large, dark mark covered his entire wrist and most of his forearm.

Kael pulled his blanket out of his bag, giving it to the laig'hius as Bridget temporarily averted her eyes. "What's your name?" Kael asked as the laig'hius jerkily pulled the blanket about him.

"I am called Phan," he rasped, his leaf-green eyes hazed with pain.

Bridget tugged on a biodegradable glove before unscrewing the bottle of orica, a new substance that aided with slowing the progression of Hemius across the body. "This will sting," she warned, "but try not to move much."

Phan shifted nervously, but he nodded. Bridget slathered the cream over the nasty bruise-like marks, and he winced in pain.

"Where is your pack?" Kael asked, distracting the laig'hius.

Phan glanced into the warped woods. "We found some ruins deeper in and took shelter there." He grimaced. "The ponds… *move*. They attacked us. Akalius, our alpha, had been dragged into the pond on our search for shelter. I was looking for food, but… I fear the worst for the rest of the pack."

Kael and Bridget exchanged glances, knowing what the other was thinking. "We'll help you save them," Bridget said firmly, wrapping Phan's Hemius wounds with bandages from her pack.

He stared at her with wide eyes. "I could not ask you to put yourself in danger like that."

"You didn't." Kael stood up, pulling out his map and checking to see how far away the ruins were. "This is part of our duty, Phan."

The laig'hius dipped his head in gratitude, his eyes closing in temporary relief. "Thank you. You have no idea how much this means to me."

"We will rest here and head out at first light," Kael planned out loud, clipping the map back together and kneeling next to Phan. He rested a hand on the laig'hius's shoulder. "We should be able to reach your comrades by nightfall if we hurry."

Phan's lupine ears twitched in anticipation. "I will guide you, then. I believe I found a relatively safe route inward, although I still need to bring food back."

"We have extra," Bridget reassured him, smiling. "They won't go hungry."

"Thank you," he murmured sincerely. "Thank you so much."

Chapter 3
Hidden

They trudged through the woods, following the limping wolf as he led them deeper and deeper into the Heramus. Luckily, they did not encounter any of the larger puddles of Hemius which could reach out and grab its prey.

Kael's eyes flitted about, watching for telltale signs of movement within the nearby Hemius. Sure, they were small, but they were often interconnected underground. One small plate-sized puddle could potentially alert the bigger ones up ahead that dinner was walking toward them.

Hemius was an insatiable, semi-intelligent monster disguised as poison.

"Kael," Bridget breathed, gesturing for him to walk alongside her. He fell in line with her stride as she continued, "If that laig'hius keeps pushing himself like that, he won't make it back to Veera."

"I think he already knows that," Kael murmured, watching the wolf. "Lupines have a fierce streak of dedication, though. We wouldn't be able to force him to abandon his pack even if we tried to."

"True." She looked uncertain. "It just feels like…"

"A trap?" he finished, and she nodded. "I understand your concern, but I do not believe that is the case. Phan is too rattled to be faking any of this."

She gave him an odd look. "All right. I trust you."

Kael quietened after seeing that look; he had seen it on so many other faces over the years. Unlike his sister, he feared his Source; he squirmed in discomfort anytime he was reminded that tiny nano-particles were living inside of him in a constant state of symbiosis. This knowledge only strengthened his resolve not to use his Source; it didn't feel like *he* was the one helping.

However, ever since he was young, he had an innate ability to tell if someone was being truthful or not. As he got older, he was able to sense other emotions and intents, such as mischief or gratitude. A traveling sorcerer had told him it was his personal Source's unique ability and he should learn to utilize it.

It scared him, though.

"Kael." Bridget's quiet voice broke him out of his brooding. She pointed ahead. "Ponds."

Phan's ears flattened against his head. A low whine came from him. *"Those are the same ones that attacked me,"* he told them, hunching next to Kael. *"The one on the far side had taken Akalius before we found the ruins."*

"How long ago was that?" Kael asked softly, kneeling next to the wolf.

"Two suns ago."

Kael's eyes flicked between the wolf and the nearest Class Five Hemius. Remembering the sounds in the forest on the first night, he frowned. "When did you find us?"

"Yesterday. Why?" The laig'hius looked at him curiously.

"… Nothing in particular." He stared at the ponds, mulling over their options. *Something else is following us*, he realized, focusing on their surroundings without turning his head.

There.

About two hundred feet behind them, he sensed a patient yet intense presence watching them. He glanced at Phan; if he was able to sense it, why not the laig'hius?

"Do you have a plan?" Bridget asked him, expectant.

"We skirt around," he responded, turning on his heel and striding directly for the presence. "Bridget, ready your weapons; we have company."

Phan sniffed at the air before releasing a discontented growl. *"My sense of smell is off; I cannot tell if enemies are nearby."*

The Hemius must be messing with his senses, Kael thought. "Less than two hundred feet in front of us is something that has been following Bridget and I for over a day, I believe. The only question is why it hasn't attacked us yet."

Phan's ears flattened against his head.

After a few minutes of walking, Kael held up a hand. Phan and Bridget stopped, holding perfectly still as the soldier tilted his head, listening.

Nothing.

Puzzled, he walked to a tree and examined the crushed grass and broken tree limbs. Phan sniffed the area, snarling, "*Something was here.*"

"Yup." Kael stood up, looking into the warped woods. "And that *something* is maintaining a safe distance from us for some reason."

"*I don't like this,*" Phan growled, baring his teeth. "*I fear it knows of the pack.*"

Kael rubbed his chin. "Possibly… it would be easier for it to find them if it followed us, after all."

"Should we take it out first, then?" Bridget asked, her gun already out and charging.

He nodded. "That's what I was thinking."

They creeped through the twisted, warped woods after the creature. However, no matter how fast or slow they moved, it kept the same distance from them. It was noon by the time they stopped for a break.

"It knows we're hunting it," Kael announced grimly.

Phan scarfed down one of the smaller rations, rejecting a second one that Bridget tried to offer him. "*The others will need it,*" he argued, turning back the way they had come from. The creature – whatever it was – seemed to be leading them farther and farther from Phan's pack.

"Kael, I don't think it's running from us," Bridget whispered, watching Phan. "I think it's a distraction."

He hesitated before nodding. "You could be right." He turned to Phan. "What do you want to do, Phan?"

"*Return to my pack*," he growled. "*I am worried that Bridget might be correct.*"

"Then we shall resume the search." Kael gestured forward. "Lead the way, friend."

Phan dipped his head respectfully, limping forward. The wolf seemed to be walking better than earlier thanks to the brief break.

Bridget walked alongside Kael, noticing his thoughtful expression. "What's on your mind?"

"It's staying a specific distance from us, yet it's still following us," he murmured. "I cannot figure out its agenda."

"Perhaps it is waiting to attack?"

"That is the most logical assumption," he admitted. "After all, I should not have been able to sense it."

"*I agree.*" Phan peered back at them, still moving forward. "*How* did *you know of it?*"

Kael shifted uncomfortably.

"Kael's Source reads the aura of those around him," Bridget explained. "It gives him the ability to sense their intent and even their emotions at times. It's how we knew you weren't leading us into a trap."

"*How interesting.*" Phan glanced at Kael, curiosity rolling off of him. "*I appreciate the trust. Thank you for helping me.*"

"No problem," Kael muttered.

"*What is wrong?*"

Bridget waved her hand dismissively. "He hates talking about it; nothing against you."

Kael turned his head away, self-conscious. Despite his loathing of his abilities, he could thank it for one thing right then.

Their stalker was getting brave, moving closer than before; it was now about a hundred and fifty feet away, and then a hundred and twenty-five feet.

A hundred and fifteen feet…

A hundred feet…

Kael whirled around, his gun aimed at where the

creature should be.

There was nothing there.

He stepped from side to side, trying to catch a glimpse through the trees. He *knew* he hadn't misjudged the distance nor the visibility. With this particular angle, he could see well over a hundred feet through the gnarly trees.

He exhaled slowly, lowering his weapon. Seeing Bridget's startled expression and Phan's raised hackles, he quickly explained, "I sensed it moving closer and thought I would be able to see it through the trees. I… guess not."

"If it comes closer, I will tear it to shreds," Phan snarled, baring his teeth.

Kael didn't holster his laser gun, but he did loosen his grip and turn the safety on. "Let's continue on. I'll keep an eye on it."

Their follower didn't come closer than one hundred feet anymore. Anytime Kael glanced behind them, he saw nothing, which was extremely disconcerting. Nothing with that large of a presence could be that small, right? He focused on the path in front of them, trying to shake his growing sense of foreboding.

A dark form oozed from behind a tree, unseen by the two patrol soldiers and the laig'hius.

Chapter 4
Dancing With Danger

Kael glanced to the side as he tracked the progress of their mysterious stalker. He turned his head when he realized it was closer than a hundred feet, but as soon as he did that, he *sensed* the panic coming off of it as it backed off.

Noticing Kael's frown, Phan asked, *"What is it doing?"*

"It is keeping pace with us," Kael murmured, his mind on overdrive. "It seems to know we know of its presence, but it is still hiding."

A sound similar to a sneeze came from the wolf. *"Sounds like a coward."*

"I agree," Bridget muttered, her hand flexing over her gun. "Ally or foe, I might just shoot it if it finally shows itself."

Kael sighed. "You are not the only one frustrated here."

She glanced at him. "It's driving you crazy, isn't it? Knowing it's back there but not being able to see it?"

"You have no clue," he grumbled, glancing behind them once again.

"We have returned." Phan stopped, baring his teeth at the pools of swirling ink. *"How are we to get around it?"*

"Skirt them," Kael stated simply, keeping his voice low. "Try to keep out of their reach. They probably have a range of ten or so feet, so we should be all right if we stick to the middle."

The wolf moved forward, but Bridget hesitated, disturbed. "How do we know they aren't just faking being inactive?" she whispered, rubbing her arm.

"We don't." Kael patted her shoulder reassuringly. "That is why we are keeping our distance."

She followed close behind him as they crept through the forest, keeping an eye on the ponds of inky Hemius that span about seven feet long. They were halfway past the second one when Phan stopped.

"*Directly ahead,*" the laig'hius warned them.

A pool of purple, red, and black ink swirled gently. A node barely rose out of the surface, bobbing this way and that.

They held perfectly still, barely breathing. Hemius hunted off of vibration and movement; if one was still enough, they could sometimes avoid detection.

The node plopped back into its puddle with barely a ripple to show its passage. The surface stilled, slowing to the point that it barely moved.

Kael exhaled slowly, attempting to calm his heart rate. He beckoned to the others, pointing down the strip of twenty feet between the black pools of liquid.

It would be cutting it close, but they had no choice.

They tiptoed between the deadly ponds, all three of them hoping that the still surfaces did not suddenly rise out of their mock-slumbers.

Noticing the gravel strewn path, Kael's jaw tensed. It was one of the Hemius's most notorious traps for its prey. He motioned to the others, alerting them of the dangerous stretch before them. They nodded in affirmation.

Kael carefully rolled his foot over the gravel, hearing it grate softly together underneath his boot. He winced, glancing between the two ponds he was currently in between.

No movement.

He took another step, and then another. He neared the end of the fourth pond where the path widened. He exhaled. *Just a little farther.*

A blackish-purple node peeked out of the left pond.

They froze. Kael stared at it, his foot raised for another step. He didn't dare set it down; any movement could set the Class Five Hemius off. He didn't even look away.

The node rose a little higher, bobbing curiously as it approached the edge of its pond. It leaned forward, touching the stones and shifting them around its border before straightening, bobbing again.

Oddly enough, Kael had a nagging suspicion the node knew something was wrong with its pathway. However, it didn't seem to be interested enough to investigate.

Kael struggled to remain still as his leg began to cramp. He needed to put it down soon, but he didn't dare do it while the Hemius was scrutinizing them to this degree.

It sank into the pond, losing interest in them. Kael slowly lowered his foot, waiting until the node was completely gone before he set it on the ground. He glanced at the others; Bridget's eyes were wide from fright while Phan trembled ever so slightly, restraining a snarl.

Kael motioned them to continue. He took a step forward.

The node burst from the surface of the pond, aiming straight for him.

He staggered back as the node barely managed to stretch far enough to pierce the ground where he had been standing. He glanced around in horror as nodes rose out of the other ponds, tilting toward them.

They ran.

It was no longer about silence and stealth; it was now about outwitting a predator that had been hunting its prey for over two thousand years.

Glimpsing the node in his peripheral, he used his next step to push himself back, barely dodging the lethal strike. His arms flailed as he regained his balance and darted around the creature's thorn-like arm.

One more, he thought grimly, seeing the last large pond ahead of them. He could only hope that the others were fairing well against the Hemius nodes.

Drawing his gun with one hand and his sword with

the other, he charged forward. As soon as the node lashed at him with its deadly precision, Kael used its own momentum against it by allowing his sword's blade to take the strike.

The purple and black spike roiled in pain, writhing in silent agony as it tried to slither away. He fired ruthlessly into the gash he had opened as Bridget and Phan rushed past him. Backing up, he followed them, firing laser shots until he was a safe distance away.

Phan whined at the Hemius slowly sinking back into its pond, the surface churning ominously. The wolf's ears flattened against his head as he hunched down, a deep growl emerging from his throat.

"We need to get out of here," Kael ordered, turning to the forest.

Bridget grabbed his arm, a look of horror on her face as she stared at the ponds. He glanced over his shoulder.

The Hemius ponds were creeping across the ground and merging together, forming a small lake over the swath of land. The trees between them creaked, crashing into the viscous liquid and sinking into the depths as through they were disintegrating.

Three nodes rose from the surface, bobbing back and forth.

A chill raced through Kael. "Run," he breathed.

They sprinted through the woods, trying to get away from the inky monster that had went from a Class Five Hemius to a Class Seven — one of the most deadliest and lethal of Hemius types inside the Heramus.

"We won't make it," Kael huffed, leaping over a fallen tree. He glanced at Phan. "You need to run faster!"

"*I… am trying,*" the injured laig'hius said, struggling to keep up. His legs gave out and he slumped to the ground, his breathing labored. He squinted in agony. "*Go on without me.*"

"I won't leave you," Kael spit through gritted teeth,

kneeling next to Phan and helping the wolf up. "Just a little farther, friend."

A whine escaped his muzzle. Phan struggled to his feet, limping forward. Kael kept pace with the wolf, keeping an eye behind them.

Black tendrils reached for them, slithering through the trees like giant snakes. The one closest to them reared up, lunging forward.

Kael raised his sword and gun, ready to fight.

The tendril stopped, straining to stretch even thinner than it already had. After a few seconds, it slowly withdrew, giving up on its prey.

Kael let his breath go, sinking to his knees next to the wolf. "We will rest here," he murmured, patting Phan's head. "We should treat your Hemius and recover."

Phan closed his eyes, leaning into Kael's hand. "*Thank you,*" he said sincerely.

Kael smiled at him. "It's what friends do."

The wolf blinked several times, startled at something. Kael sensed a brief flicker of recognition in the wolf's emotions. "*Indeed it is, old friend.*"

Chapter 5
Living Nightmare

Kael glanced at the sky, growing worried. "We should stop for the night," he recommended, pausing by a gnarly tree. They had been traveling for the day, but now warm splashes of color were painting the sky.

Phan stared at him incredulously. He was in his bipedal form and wearing a spare set of Kael's clothes. His left arm was in a sling fashioned out of dead wood and bandages. "We are just a moonrise away from them. If we keep pushing forward – "

"It is dangerous to travel the Heramus at night." Kael set his bag down, checking his belt and the charge on his laser gun. "The Hemius enters a constant state of activity as soon as the sun sets. Stay here; I will scout around and ensure this is a safe location to post camp."

"Allow me to accompany you," Phan requested, stepping forward.

Kael shook his head. "No; stay with Bridget." He had already told them of the return of their mysterious follower, but he hoped to draw it out if he went on his own.

"How's your flare gun?" Bridget asked, already pulling out camping gear. "Does it need any maintenance?"

He pulled out the contraption, examining the barrel in the dying light. He clicked the power on, checking the cooling elements. "Looks good for this patrol. I'll sterilize it when I get back."

She nodded, withdrawing a rod from her bag. Setting it on the ground, she pressed a few buttons and backed up as it extended in a circle, forming a basic barrier around the small camp. "I'll leave it transparent until you return."

"Got it." He set out, using his map to walk a wide circle around their temporary camp.

He notated a few puddles and small ponds on the map for reference tomorrow, but he didn't see any Class Four or higher ponds. Completing his circuit, he sighed in relief; they should be safe for the night. Turning toward the camp, he suddenly sensed a spike of intent.

Whirling around, he scanned the forest for the creature that had been following them. "I know you're there," he called out, his hand wrapping around his gun. "Quit hiding."

A low snarl drifted over the breeze from the direction of the stalking creature.

He pulled out his sword and flipped off the safety on his gun. "Aren't you sick of hiding?" he cajoled.

The presence faded as it put some distance between itself and him. He frowned, straightening. Why did it run? What was its objective?

Puzzled, he returned to the makeshift camp. Bridget looked up from the Source fire she had started. "How was it?"

"We should be all right here," he murmured, sitting next to the still-bipedal Phan. He pulled out his laser gun, checking the gears as he chatted with the laig'hius. "How's your arm?"

"Better," he admitted, smiling sheepishly. "I… never even thought to switch to my bipedal form to allow it to rest."

"I assume you stay predominantly in your lupine form?" he asked as he dug in his pack, withdrawing a small cleaning kit. He sprayed the gun down before wiping the sterilizing agent off with a rubbery cloth.

He nodded. "We only switch to the bipedal form when our lupine form causes more inconveniences than not; only Akalius and I are fully used to our bipedal forms." His expression darkened. "Now that Akalius is gone, though, I will have to take over the pack."

Putting the gun away, Kael patted Phan's shoulder.

"You will do great," he encouraged the laig'hius. "Your dedication to the pack shows, Phan. You will be a great leader."

He shook his head. "The title should go to Akalius's mate, Uri. However, he was grieving, so I took over to keep the pack from falling apart."

Kael's eyebrows raised in surprise. "The alpha was female? Isn't that rare?"

"She was the strongest," Phan clarified. "We do not judge based off of sex, just strength and intelligence. She was the best out of all of us."

Kael's gaze dropped to the fake flames. "My condolences for your loss," he murmured, feeling guilty at not saying it earlier.

"She is in Eleth now," Phan said with a smile. "Free from pain. It is for the best."

Kael briefly closed his eyes. "Indeed. Get some rest, my friend; we shall make it to your pack tomorrow."

Phan stretched out on the ground. Bridget glanced at Kael staring into the Source generated flames. "You should get some rest, too, Kael. I'll take the first watch."

He sighed. "Will do. Thank you, Bridget."

He rested on his side, his back facing the warm Source flames. However, he did not get a wink of sleep that night; the creature lurking just out of sight kept him up, and even when they switched watch, he didn't grow tired.

Their stalker was getting hungry.

When they rose the next day, Kael took a portion of his rations and placed it on the ground. Phan and Bridget watched him curiously.

"What was that for?" Bridget asked as they continued through the woods.

"Our mysterious friend," Kael responded, glancing over his shoulder. "It is getting hungry, and I fear its passive, observant state might shift. I figured if we could sate it at least a little bit, maybe it will maintain its distance."

"Or perhaps it will attack once it is stronger," Phan argued, his lips curling upward. Despite being in his bipedal form, it looked very much like a wolf's snarl. "I would have let it starve."

Bridget glanced at the silent Kael. "Surely, you knew of this risk," she murmured.

"I did." He adjusted his hand on his laser gun. "While I was scouting last night, it got closer than any other time. However, even when I taunted it, it did not come out."

Phan shot him a disapproving look. "It is good that it did not, as I fear it would have torn you apart."

"We don't even know what it is," Kael pointed out. Feeling a change in the presence behind them, he glanced back. "It seems as though it found the food."

Bridget glanced behind them, unnerved. "What does it even want? I don't understand why it's following us this far."

"I don't know." Kael admitted. He glanced back, startled as he felt the presence rapidly approaching with renewed focus – and an intent to kill. "Carc'ra. Change of plans!"

He whipped out his gun, pointing it in the direction of the mystery creature. Bridget followed his guidance, aiming hers in the same direction.

Kael tracked the creature, keeping his gun steady. A large, black form zipped through the trees, too fast to make it out as it took a wide arc around them and… kept going.

"The pack!" Phan growled.

They rushed forward, chasing after the thing that had been following them just moments before.

Seeing a dark mound ahead, Kael stopped, thrusting his arm out to halt Bridget. Creeping forward, he covered his nose at the awful smell of rotting meat as he identified the shape.

An infected kranluk rested on the ground, old blood

staining the dead grass. It must have died a few hours ago, and something had already eaten half of it.

Bridget glanced around, unsettled. "Where did it go?"

"We are near the pack," Phan said, alarmed. "We need to – "

"It's still here," Kael whispered, scanning the trees. He saw a sliver of black disappear behind the largest warped tree. Training his gun on it, he called out, "We know you're there. Come out, or I will shoot."

A black blob flowed out from behind the tree, rising to stand eight feet tall. It stared at Kael with bloody red eyes, its maul opening to reveal rows upon rows of sharp teeth stained with old blood. It growled menacingly, slithering forward as two blobs protruded from its midsection, forming arms that reached for them.

It was a night terror.

He stumbled backward, his eyes wide with horror. Nightmare creatures were from Carni, the realm between worlds, and were never allowed in the material realms. Why was this one here?!

The creature stared at him, curling its lipless mouth back to expose its rows of sharp, pointed teeth.

It roared, lunging toward them.

Chapter 6
Lyra

They staggered back, but the night terror was too fast. Kael closed his eyes, waiting for the blow that would send him to the Elethavi. *I love you, Clarissa,* he thought.

Crunch.

Peering out of a slit eye, Kael blinked rapidly in stunned surprise as the night terror ate the carcass, bones and all.

Bridget creeped next to him, hissing, "Let's get out of here while it's distracted!"

They hurried away, slipping around the huge monster from a different realm. Kael glanced back in time to see the night terror pause in its meal. It watched them leave before returning to its lunch.

"What was that?" Phan asked, his voice shaking.

"A night terror." Bridget glanced at Kael. "Right?"

He nodded, giving Phan a brief explanation. "It's a nightmare-class creature from Carni. They are manifested from people's worst dreams and nightmares; they aren't allowed in any of the realms, though."

Phan paused, glancing back. "Don't you need to stop it, then?"

Kael shook his head. "Our weapons are not designed for killing night terrors." He exhaled in a huff. "At least now we know why it was keeping its distance."

"Why?" The laig'hius glanced behind them once again.

"They feed mostly off of fear and tension," he informed the nervous lupine. "By keeping a set distance from its target, it can feed off the tension and anxiety of its prey but also stay safely away in case the prey tries to retaliate. They may look terrifying, but that is only to instill fear so it may feed off the emotion."

"How would you explain that carcass, then, bookworm?" Bridget demanded, her nerves still rattled.

"By what I remember, they need substance to maintain their form." He racked his brain; the books that his tutor had him study were from several years ago. "They… they usually just devour whatever is lying around. Eating living things is normally too much trouble."

Unless it's starving. He kept this part to himself, not wanting to freak out his companions any more than they already were. Sparing a look behind them, he now saw the night terror following them, its teeth still holding the shredded remains of the dead kranluk.

He couldn't help the spike of fear that rushed through him when it clicked its teeth together.

Bridget squeaked in terror when she noticed the nightmare creature. "It's already done?!"

Kael gritted his teeth. "Bridget, it won't hurt us!" Based off its size, that kranluk should sate its corporeal needs for a week or so. That would give them plenty of time to rescue the lupine laig'hius pack and leave.

"I didn't sign up for this," she moaned, keeping up with the jogging laig'hius in front.

Phan slowed down, glancing back at the night terror with narrowed eyes. "You are sure it will not attack?"

Kael paused. "I am not an expert," he admitted slowly. "But by what I *do* know of them, just our fear and tension should keep it at bay."

"It definitely has *me* terrified," Bridget muttered darkly.

And I am sure it is enjoying the meal, Kael thought to himself, glimpsing the night terror through the trees. Just as he suspected, it is keeping its distance – scare tactics 101.

Phan mulled over it for a brief moment before moving forward. "I will trust you, Kael," he said, his green eyes flicking to the soldier. "But if it attacks, I expect you to help me protect my pack."

"Of course I will."

Within minutes, they approached an especially large,

hollowed-out tree. On the other side of it, Kael could see the fallen structures of the old city that had stood here before Ecalain War II that had created the Heramus.

A hand curled around the edge of the hollowed entrance. Two yellow eyes peered out, blonde hair shifting over twitching lupine ears. The little lupine girl shrieked in excitement at the sight of Phan, leaping out and hugging him tightly. Kael quickly averted his gaze from the child no more than nine years old, mentally reminding himself that most laig'hius, especially the young ones, do not know the social customs of wearing clothes.

"Phan, you're back!" the little girl exclaimed, her arms wrapped tightly around Phan's leg. She beamed up at him.

He gave her an irritated look. "Lyra, what have I told you about shifting?"

She pouted, stepping back from him. Her form shifted and molded into a gold-furred pup that crouched in excitement. "*Did you bring food? I'm so hungry!*"

"Settle down, Lyra." He glanced at Bridget and Kael, his eyes pleading. "Could you…?"

"Of course," Bridget reassured him, taking off her bag. Phan led her inside the hollow tree.

Kael leaned against the entrance, keeping a watchful eye on the surroundings. He caught glimpses of the night terror, but it did not draw close enough to elicit concern.

Feeling a tug at his belt pouch, he looked down to see the same girl from before. This time, though, she was wearing one of Bridget's undershirts; it hung down to the girl's knees. "Are you an Alkinian, mister?" she asked, her gold-furred ears twitching in curiosity as she stared at his ears.

He knelt so he was on the same eye level as the little laig'hius. Glancing inside the oversized hollow tree, he saw Phan and Bridget in the middle of a pack of four wolves chowing on the quick, simple meals. "I am, mostly. Didn't Phan tell you not to use your bipedal form?"

"The lady gave me this!" Lyra exclaimed, twisting in the oversized shirt. "Phan is all right with me being in this form as long as I wear fabric."

Kael couldn't help the small chuckle. "Have you eaten yet?"

She nodded exuberantly, grinning at him. "Hey, mister. Your eyes remind me of someone I knew a looooong time ago."

"Is that so?" Amused, he leaned his back against the entrance, sitting cross-legged.

"Yeah!" She sat next to him, kicking her bare feet against the ground. "He used to be a guard, and I used to be an ambassador!"

His lips quirked up. The little pup had an extravagant imagination. "Sounds like you had an important role."

"I did!" Eyeing the cylindrical map poking out of his back pouch, she snatched it and opened it. "Oooh, this is so cool! Is this where we are? What are these little lines?"

Kael laughed. The little girl's excitement and innocence was a welcome change to the gloomy, somber atmosphere of the Heramus. "The lines are where Phan, Bridget, and I have been. We're currently near the middle of the Heramus, which is a scary place on Blazhreia."

Her yellow lupine eyes met his sky blue ones. "Is that why you're here, mister? Are you going to rescue us?"

His heart twisted; he had always had a soft spot for children. His own sister used to have that same look on her face before she had lost her best friend to a Hemius infection. "Of course," he murmured. "I'll make sure you make it out alive."

"You won't die, will you, mister?" Her eyes welled up. He was about to respond when she continued, "I don't want you to die again."

A chill raced down his spine.

"Lyra, what are you doing?" Phan huffed, turning to Kael. "I apologize, Kael; she has an inquisitive spirit."

"It's quite all right," Kael brushed off, smiling as Lyra scampered to Bridget who gave the young pup another meal packet. "She was cute."

Phan watched her rip the packet open, chewing on the tough jerky inside. "Do you have children?"

"I wish!" Kael laughed. "My betrothed and I are looking forward to it when we're married. We both want a child. We already have a few favorite names, too."

Phan relaxed a little, smiling at him. "You cannot always choose the name before the child comes, though; take Lyra. She may be young in body, but she has an old soul." He scrutinized Kael's face. "She said something to you, didn't she?"

"She has a wild imagination," Kael commented. "She thought I was a guard from a different time."

"I… suppose so." The look Phan gave him suddenly made the soldier doubt his own words.

Chapter 7
Crystal Shells

Lyra swung her arms about herself, enjoying the walk. Phan sighed, exasperated at the pup who refused to follow instructions. "Lyra, you need to stay with your father."

She puffed out her cheeks rebelliously. "No. I want to walk with Kael."

Kael glanced down at her, amused. Ever since they had started their trek that morning, the pup hadn't left his side. Not that he minded, though; he was used to children taking with him easily.

"Kael, Kael." Lyra stared up at him and tugged on his sleeve. "Do you have any brothers or sisters?"

"I have a little sister," he told her, allowing her to hold his hand. "She's fourteen now, but I've always taken care of her." *In fact, she is probably getting a little too old for me to continue helping her with everything.* He glanced at the little wolf-girl in the oversized shirt. *She reminds me so much of Kimala...*

Yellow eyes met his. Her gold-haired ears tilted back. "Kael, why are you sad?"

He blinked, startled. "Just thinking," he murmured, glancing around. "Phan, how is our course?"

The bipedal laig'hius pulled out Kael's map, examining their progress. "We should be skirting the Class Seven Hemius soon."

Kael nodded; the plan was to walk around the oversized Hemius pond, keeping the pack as safe as possible as they worked their way out of the Heramus. This route would take longer, but safety was a priority.

Bridget jogged through the trees, returning from a scouting mission. A white wolf kept pace with her. Expression grim, she reported, "Kael, there's a major problem up ahead."

A groan slipped past his lips. There was *always* a problem. "Out with it."

It was the white wolf, Uri, who responded. *"There is a large pond within range on our route. We will be going between the two Hemius ponds just up ahead."*

"Carc'ra," Kael swore under his breath. He glanced over the pack, his jaw tensing. "Bridget."

"Yeah, partner?"

"Get out the crystal shots; we're going in specter."

She straightened her stance at the order. "Understood."

Phan and Uri watched them, curious. Lyra cooed over Kael's bag as Phan asked, "What does that mean? Is it a Blazhreian phrase?"

"It's used in the patrol units of the city," Bridget explained, carefully pulling out a container. Inside, the multifaceted orbs were cushioned and protected from being jostled. "It means we will be stealthy. Not only that, but our most lethal, powerful weapons are used first instead of as a last resort."

Kael flipped open the lid to his own case of crystal shots. At Lyra's twinkling eyes, he smiled and handed her one of the orbs.

Phan stared at the exchange, too stunned to stop it. "I-is that safe?" he asked, watching Lyra twist the orb about so it reflected the light brightly.

"It is harmless until it's put into one of these." He loaded five sparkling orbs into the usually empty chamber of the laser gun's handle. "They require mixed Voyana and Source to activate, and then keeps them under pressure until it fires. They explode on impact, dealing shards into its target."

Phan and Uri stared at him, their eyes wide at the description. Lyra looked between his gun and the orb he had given her. "Here," she offered, holding up the orb. "You can have it back."

"Keep it," Kael encouraged, smiling at her. "Just be careful; it's fragile."

She nodded, her fingers curling around it.

He clipped the small container to his belt for easy reloading access before standing up. Screwing on the barrel needed to properly fire the crystal shells, he nodded to Bridget. "Take the rear. Phan, stay with me; Uri, go with Bridget."

Bridget nodded, falling behind the group. Uri followed her, grumbling in discontent at being sent to the back of the pack.

Phan followed close to Kael, watching the soldier out of the corner of his eye. "This plan – "

"It will work."

Lyra grabbed his hand. "Kael," she whimpered, her eyes wide with fear. "I don't want you to fight."

He knelt in front of her, giving her a reassuring smile. "Remember when you asked me if I was going to rescue you?"

"Uh-huh."

"This is me doing that." He rubbed the top of her head, tousling her hair. "But I need you to do something for me, Lyra. If things ever get scary or dangerous, run as fast as you can."

"But – "

"Will you promise me?"

Her eyes dropped to the ground. "I promise," she whispered.

He patted the top of her head. "We'll protect you, Lyra. Go to your Aunt Shurivurra now."

Lyra ran up to the gold, red, and brown female wolf. She nuzzled the girl, trying to get her to transform, but the pup was stubborn in her decision to stick to a bipedal form.

Now that Lyra was with the rest of the pack, Kael murmured to Phan, "I want you to use this in the fight."

He offered his sword to him.

The laig'hius shook his head. "I have my own talons and teeth." He gave Kael a sad smile. "I fear I will not make it after this battle, anyway."

"Do not say that, friend. Medical knowledge has advanced significantly since the opening of Cerlail Academy; you still have a chance."

"Thank you for the encouragement." Taking a deep breath, he winced. "Let us see how much more this body can take."

Kael shot the laig'hius a sidelong glance. He knew the bipedal was hiding his injuries so the pack didn't panic; Kael could only imagine what kind of pain he was in right now.

He touched his hip, thinking of the tincture Kimala had given him. It would have been created under the supervision of Medic Surv, her mentor and the best medic in Veera. The effects would be legitimate; the medic advisor wouldn't allow Kimala to take home a prototype that didn't work. Perhaps —

"Save it for the others," Phan murmured. Kael glanced at him, startled. "Bridget told me about it, but I requested her not to ask you for it. If I die protecting the pack, it will be an honorable death."

Kael took a deep breath. "I will fight by your side and get you out of here, Phan," he said, his voice firm.

Phan laughed, patting Kael's shoulder. "Then perhaps we are all getting out of here! After all, the mighty — "

Boom.

"Kael!" Bridget yelled, the smoke from the shot clearing to reveal a writhing tendril of Hemius. The wolves hunched in fear, surrounding Lyra protectively.

Without another word, Kael raised his weapon and fired two rounds of the crystal shrapnel into the Class Seven Hemius. It reared back in pain.

Phan knocked into him, pushing him aside as another

tendril from the opposite direction dug into the ground.

"Carc'ra," he breathed, scrambling to his feet as Phan shifted into his lupine form. "They're *both* awake."

The laig'hius tossed the discarded clothes at Uri, the cylindrical map quickly following it. *"Uri, take Lyra and run!"* Phan ordered.

Within seconds, Uri was in his bipedal form and tugging on the clothes. His white hair tumbled about as he scooped Lyra up and took off, the rest of the pack following him.

"No! Kael!" Lyra screamed, reaching over Uri's shoulder for the soldier. "Kael!"

Kael's heart wrenched at her desperate cries. For a brief moment, he felt as if someone had called out to him like that before. Shaking off the déjà vu feeling, he fired at the tendrils following the pack.

"No!" Lyra screamed one last time. "No, Uri, go back! We have to save Cain!"

Distracted, Kael glanced at Lyra. The name was not his, but it sounded similar; the last letter was what made the difference. The oddest part, though, was the feeling that he should know that name.

"Kael, watch out!" Bridget shouted, shoving him to the side just as the spear shaped tendril pierced where he had been.

Where Bridget was now.

She reflexively grabbed at the purplish-black spear, crying out in pain as her bare hands were burned by the solidified, poisonous substance. She struggled to breathe as her body slumped over the tendril. Her eyes glazed over as she stared at Kael.

"Kill… these cavu," she rasped, blood trickling out of her mouth.

The tendril snaked around her leisurely. She screamed at the new contact, but the Hemius soon encapsulated her, muffling the sound.

Kael gritted his teeth, glaring at the Hemius as he blinked to clear his blurring vision. He took a ragged breath, his thoughts swirling; Class Seven Hemius was difficult to drive off. It was the same class as the lakes in the ruins, which were always awake, and one down from the Hemius monsters that could walk.

"Kael." Phan stood with his back to his pack and was snarling protectively. *"Go; protect them."*

Kael glanced behind them. The pack was already past the dangerous zone, still running. "They're safe. I will stay and fight with you, friend."

Phan dipped his head in respect. *"Thank you."*

They stood ready, facing the approaching Hemius with heads held high.

Chapter 8
The Selfless Soldier

Kael fired one shot after another, keeping the Hemius at bay as they slowly backed up. The one that had devoured Bridget was slowly dragging itself through the woods, already sated with its prey while the rest of the tendrils continued hunting.

Kael flipped open his side pouch, popping five crystal orbs into his gun. Phan leaped forward and snarled menacingly, swiping his already-infected paw at the Hemius. It reared back in pain before lunging at the wolf.

Boom, boom, boom.

The man and wolf each took a few steps back, putting more distance between them and the lethal Hemius tendrils.

"Kael, behind us!" Phan warned.

Kael whirled around, leaping out of the way just in time. The tendril grazed his armored jacket, slowing it enough so it only sliced the metal and not his skin.

Tossing the ruined material to the side, he fired his last two shots into the tendril before quickly flipping open the underside of the handle and popping another five orbs into the chamber. A pained yelp had him twisting around to see Phan collapsed on the ground, a tendril coiled for the final strike.

Kael aimed, not even flinching at the explosive sounds his gun made as he fired a shot into all five of the surrounding tendrils. Pulling the giant wolf upright, he urged the laig'hius forward as he reloaded his gun once again.

A tendril raced for him just as he latched the chamber closed.

Phan slammed into him, pushing him back. It was not enough, though.

The tendril pierced through his thin shirt, planting a searing kiss on his chest as it reached its limit of reach. He grunted in pain, firing twice.

The tendril reared back.

Kael grasped his shirt in his fist, sucking in one breath after another as he and Phan staggered away. After several yards, the pain was too much; Kael collapsed, curling into a ball as his fist clenched over his chest.

Phan whimpered, nuzzling Kael's reddened face. "*Kael, take the antidote.*"

Kael shook his head. "No, Phan. You – "

"*I have already said my parting words,*" Phan cut him off. "*Your family does not even know. You need to return to them.*"

Kael stared at the laig'hius, his eyes glazing in pain as his vision blurred. "I-I can't…"

He literally couldn't; the single touch of Hemius was a writhing, expanding blossom of fire in his chest. If it touched his heart –

A bottle pressed to his lips, and a sweet liquid poured into his mouth. He swallowed reflexively, nearly choking as even more replaced it. He stared up at Phan's determined, fierce expression.

"You will live, Kael," he said firmly as the soldier finished off the bottle.

Kael coughed, his hand clenching over the Hemius. However, as the seconds ticked by, the pain abated as the Hemius grew still, sedated for the time being.

He took one shaky breath after another, his clenched fingers slowly relaxing. He gazed at Phan, amazed. "It… worked," he whispered, laughing incredulously. He had thought for sure that he was too far gone for it to be effective, but here he was, still alive. "My little sister's tincture worked."

Phan frowned. "Your… sister's?" Shaking his head, he dispelled his curiosity. Exhausted, he shifted back into the form he was most comfortable with. "*You need to leave,*

Kael."

"You're coming with me," Kael argued, kneeling in front of the exhausted wolf. "We're going to get you fixed up, too."

Phan didn't respond, but he limped alongside Kael. Despite their pace, they made decent progress through the Heramus, making it to their old campsite just after nightfall.

"Just… a couple hours," Kael mumbled, leaning against a tree. He glanced at Phan in concern, noticing his friend's labored breathing. "How are you doing?"

"*Never better.*" Phan's eyes closed as he stretched out on the ground. "*It was good fighting with you again.*"

Kael shook his head. "We've never fought together before today, though."

"*Not in this lifetime.*" One green eye peered at him. "*I suppose I could meet you again at the Elethavi. I am sure the Death'Lord will allow that, at least.*"

Alarm shot through Kael, making his chest twinge as the Hemius mildly reacted. "Don't say that," he ordered. "We'll make it, Phan. We just need to get to the border so Veera can see my flare."

"*It is too late for me, old friend.*" Phan's eyes slid closed, not reopening this time. "*Thank you for protecting my family.*"

"Phan, you need to stay awake." The wolf didn't respond. "Phan. Phan!"

Crawling to the wolf, Kael pressed his cheek against the wolf's side.

Nothing.

Kael's vision blurred. "Thana baro, Phan," he breathed, resting his hand on the wolf's head for a brief moment as he whispered the Alkinian words for 'safe travels.' Hot tears struck the wolf's fur as he mourned for his friends that had been lost in the battle.

He walked throughout the night, his chest aching from more than just the Hemius's touch now. He stumbled over branches and rocks; he leaned against trees for brief respites. He could sense the night terror still following him, but he just couldn't bring himself to care anymore.

The sun was just rising over the horizon as his foot encountered green grass. He fell to his knees, staring at his hands.

You need to return to them. Phan's words rang through his head. His hand moved on its own, pulling out his gun. He loaded it with a single flare shot and pointed it upward.

Zzzzz... ching!

His sky blue Source colored flare exploded in the warm sky, lingering in the air to mark his location. Collapsing on his back, he stared up at the pretty blue flakes floating above him.

He closed his eyes, thinking to rest for just a minute. However, someone shook his shoulder after what felt like only seconds had passed.

"Kael," Royce breathed, looking as if he had seen a ghost. He was one of the guards from Veera; Kael had occasionally patrolled the city with him. "You're still alive."

"Bridget... Bridget didn't make it," Kael croaked. Royce pressed water to his lips, and he drank a large gulp.

Royce's partner, Rick, stretched out a mobile medical cot. "Let's get him on this and head back," he advised.

Kael rolled onto the cot, stretching out and wincing slightly. Rick pressed a few buttons along the side bar, and within seconds, the cot slowly rose to hip-height. Rick and Royce walked on either side of it, guiding the medical unit through the woods.

Kael fell in and out of consciousness throughout the trip to Veera. When they made it back to the medical facility, he couldn't help the sheepish grin as he was greeted by Medic Surv, Kimala's tutor and mentor.

"How are you still alive?" Surv breathed, his eyes wide as he inspected Kael's wound.

"Kimala's tincture," the soldier admitted, wincing as

he sat up. "It stopped the movement almost completely."

Surv's eyes grew even wider. "It's a miracle," he murmured. "When did you receive the wound?"

"Midday yesterday," he reported. "It was a Class Seven Hemius." He glanced at the door. "Can I… see my family?"

"You should not move," Surv warned him, digging in the drawers. "Carc'ra… we're out of the infusion cylinders."

"Surv." The old medic paused, glancing at the solemn young man. "Please get my family and Clarissa."

Surv slowly exhaled, slumping against the medical supply drawers. "If that is what you wish."

"It is." He gave the medic a shaky smile. "We both know I won't make it after this wears off. I want to be able to say goodbye properly."

Surv stared at him for a moment before nodding. "I will send a messenger."

The next hour was the most precious to Kael. His adventures through the Heramus faded away as he comforted his crying sister and parents. He talked to Codi, asking him to take care of his little sister, which sent his cousin over the edge.

When Clarissa walked in hurt the most.

She had already been crying; her makeup was smeared, her cheeks were bright red, and she was still wearing the apron from the bakery. She collapsed against him, wailing and begging him to tell her that none of it was true.

He stroked her hair, squeezing his eyes shut tightly as he whispered the words he had wanted to tell her ever since he knew he would die. "I love you, Clarissa, but even more than that, I want you to be happy." He kissed her cheek. "You have a beautiful mind; share it with others."

She choked on a sob, refusing to leave his side.

The small room remained crowded throughout the rest of the day and into the night. When the Hemius began to move again, not even the full dose of anti-Hemius pills slowed it. Surv drove out the family, not wanting them to remember their son like this. Clarissa was the hardest to convince; Jonan and Codi had to drag her out of the room.

Surv sat in the seat next to Kael, clasping his clammy hand. The young man gave him a pained smile. "Thank… you, Surv," he forced out.

He stared at Kael, helpless. "I wish I could help you," he admitted.

"It's… all right." Kael leaned back, his jaw tightening as he felt the Hemius constricting around vital organs. "They're… safe, and that's… all that matters."

"Who?" Surv asked. Kael had said it had been a Class Seven Hemius that had caught him and Bridget, but he never explained why the two of them were that deep inside the cursed region.

"The… pack. They were trapped." Kael stared at the ceiling, his eyes glazing over as he breathed, "I apologize, Lyra."

Surv dipped his head in respect.

Kael's hand loosened, falling to his side.

To this day, Medic Surv had not told a soul of the last words uttered by the soldier; he had believed the poor young man had been delirious in his last hours, as the name he had spoken was that of an ancient laig'hius ambassador from thousands of years ago when the Ecalain had been a powerful influence over the realms.

And thus, no one ever knew that Kael Brunet had rescued the reincarnation of the ambassador of the Alamir family, who now waited patiently for the Alamiran Ecalain to return to the land.

Epilogue

Kael blinked, his vision slowly returning. He stared at the huge gate in front of him, a little stunned.

Elethavi was bigger than he expected.

"Kael."

His gaze dropped to find Phan in his bipedal form standing in front of the closed monolithic gate. He grinned, stepping toward his new friend. "It is good to see you again."

Phan tilted his head to the side, puzzled. "If you say so. Were you able to reunite with your family?"

Kael sobered. "Yes. They were sad, but… I feel as if being able to say goodbye was good for them."

"Phan, is this who you were waiting for?" someone murmured in surprise.

Kael glanced to the left. A man about his age stood near one of the grey pillars, his bronze hair messy and his jade-green eyes glinting in recognition. A black cloak edged in gold covered his clothes. The image of a gold-outlined gate rested over his left breast, and plated armor held the cloak on his shoulders.

"Eleth'Lord?" Kael breathed the respectful title of the Highlord, one of the individuals with a duty to keep the balance between the realms; this particular Highlord watched over the multi-realm prison system that held the worst criminals in existence. He bowed deeply. "It is an honor to meet you in person."

The Eleth'Lord gave the young man a smile. "It is my pleasure, as well. Phan requested to wait to go through the Gate until you were here."

Phan slowly shifted into his wolf form, his black fur sleek and unmarred by Hemius. *"Shall we go through together?"*

Kael laughed, feeling the anxiety of entering Eleth – the death realm – dissipating. "I will gladly accompany you, friend."

The large stone gate groaned as it opened to reveal the forest just outside of Veera; the colors were muted, almost grey, but Kael still recognized it. They walked through together without hesitation.

⎯⎯⎯⎯⎯◆⎯⎯⎯⎯⎯

Lyra sniffled, staring at the pretty crystal orb wrapped in leather. "They're back together, Uri," she whispered, burying her face into her father's fur coat. She clenched Bridget's shirt to herself, unwilling to return to her lupine form at the risk of losing the first gifts she had received.

The orb glistened around her neck. She swore to herself that she would tell the story of Phan and Kael for the rest of her life to anyone who would listen.

LANGUAGE DICTIONARY

If you would like a pronunciation guide, please go online to the Danarko Vault:
www.maxinastoribrook.com

Akalius	Storm.
Alamir	The name of the most popular, historical Ecalain family; they had built Alamirana and had been a prominent figurehead for centuries.
Alamiran Ecalain	The residing Ecalain over Alamirana, the City of Energized Glass.
Alkina	Home world of the Alkinian (elf) species and Voyana.
Alkinian	The predominant species that lives on Alkina; also known as elves.
Blazhreia	Home world of Blazhreians and the country of Saheir. It is much like Earth in size; however, due to Alkinian influence, its technological advancements are drastically different.

Blazhreian	The term that is used to refer to someone from Blazhreia. Also used to differentiate between a word classified as Common (an accepted cross-realm language) or a word native to this specific world.
By the Flow	An exclamatory phrase in reference to the flow of Voyana.
Carc'ra	Kranluk manure. It is used as an interjection.
Carni	The realm between all of the other known realms. | Add'l Names: Corridor Realm; Dream Realm
Cavu	A derogative word that literally translates to "invalid" or "worthless" when referencing or speaking directly to someone. It is an insulting term.
Cerlail Academy	An academy specifically designed to provide a central location for everything learned about Voyana and Source in order to more efficiently put it to use.
Death'Lord	The Common title of the Highlord who oversees Hariana and Ele-

Death'Lord (cont.)	thanos. See Eleth'Lord.
Ecalain	Spokesperson (Old Xharos). They are known as individuals who can speak with Voyana and control Source better than the average person. Entire books have been written around the definition of an Ecalain and who they are in history.
Ecalain War II	In Blaz Yr 4267, the Da'ruha and that century's Ecalain had waged war. Where they had fought is now the Heramus, and Hemius is a by-product of that war.
Eleth	Death Realm. All who are deceased go here. | Note: "Realm" is used even though this is common improper terminology. It should be "Death Dimension."
Eleth'Lord	Death'Lord. This is the Xharos title for the Highlord who watches Elethanos and Elethavi, ensuring the dead do not encroach on the living realms as well as keeping an eye on the Da'ruha. Also called the Death'Lord.
Elethavi	Death Gate. This is the barrier between Elethanos and Eleth.

Flare Gun	A contraption similar in shape to Earth's pistol. However, it does not shoot physical projectiles; instead, it gathers the owner's Source and mixes it with Voyana in a way where it will explode in mid-air regardless of the user's Source level or experience. The explosion is relatively harmless and often used as a distress signal.
Guldon	An aquatic animal on Alkina; has six fins that propel it through the thick waters.
Hemius	Living Curse Poison. It is a viscous Source fueled liquid that kills its victims.
Heramus	Living Curse Scar. A section of land to the west of Veera infected with Hemius puddles that had been the result of Ecalain War II.
Highlord	A group of authorities that keep peace between the realms and defend against realm-level catastrophes, such as the Da'ruha.
Laig'hius	A creature from Saronis that has the ability to switch between two forms: an animal form and a humanoid

Laig'hius	form. Oftentimes, the humanoid form contains characteristics of the animal form.
Lyra	Music.
Mindspeech	A method of communication; the speaker uses their Source to directly communicate to the listener's Source. Anyone ranked 5 or higher in Source can learn this ability, though it is not that common of a technique outside of government or higher officials aside from laig'hius and other shapeshifting creatures.
Narein	One of the two moons of Blazhreia.
Naros	One of the two moons of Blazhreia.
Night Terror	A nightmare-class creature from Carni that is the manifestation of people's nightmares. This particular type usually only feeds off of a person's fear, so it will use scare tactics in order to feed. Rarely, it needs physical substance in order to maintain its physical form.
Nightmare-Class Creature	A type of creature from Carni; this class is "born" from the terrors

Nightmare-Class Creature (cont.)	within people's nightmares and ill wishes.
Orica	Hemius ointment; it numbs pain and slows down the spread of infection.
Phan	Shadow.
Quasala	The capital of Saheir and the fourth-largest city.
Saheir	A country in the northern hemisphere of Blazhreia; it is a large island with a mountain range in the north and coasts in the south, with fields and forests in the middle. Only a thin strip of land connect it to Garnesh, which is four times bigger than Saheir.
Source	Voyana that has fused to the genetic code of an individual.
Specter (Combat Style)	A type of combat style refined within Saheir that refers to soldiers using stealth and assassination tactics to reach their objective. Hit fast and hard. Noise is kept to a minimum.

Shurivurra	Dawnrunner.
Thana Baro	Safe Travels.
Uri	Fang.
Veera	Fifth-largest city in Saheir; also one of the easternmost cities from the capital, Quasala. This is where Kimala was born and raised.
Voyana	Energy (Old Xharos) | It is a bio-chemical that devours chemicals and hazardous fumes in the atmosphere that would otherwise kill life. It developed sentience upon being introduced to the atmosphere 6,000 years ago. Those genetically affected by its presence can utilize it as an external energy source.
Xharos	The Alkinian language; used as both a spoken language and a way to focus Source. While the runes are no longer used in daily writing, they are still utilized in Source and Voyana techniques.

Day		Month
Zanuni	Monday	Tora
Bruanuni	Tuesday	Eona
Denuni	Wednesday	Vuva
Koranuni	Thursday	Sona
Wionuni	Friday	Maua
Senuni	Saturday	Kenza
Xhenuni	Sunday	Alona
		Rawa
		Pina

Season		
Torakonu	Summer	Lefa
Sonakonu	Fall	Fua
Alorakonu	Winter	Zua
Fuakonu	Spring	Owa

* Seven days in a week, four weeks in a month, thirteen months in a year.

Check out the Danarko Vault online for more content. It contains an extensive language dictionary with pronunciation guides, character and world information, and more.
www.maxinastoribrook.com

WANT MORE CONTENT?

Maxina has put much love and effort into this series. She has created an entire website dedicated to the languages, characters, and worlds called the *Danarko Vault*. It is accessible through her main website:

www.maxinastoribrook.com

Maxina also has a Patreon where she posts exclusive short stories, alternate perspectives, novelettes, and even chapters of books she is writing. Patrons get special behind-the-scenes look at her writing, art, and future projects.

The *Sealed Archives*, a Patreon-exclusive website, is treated like the archives of Maxina's Patreon, making it a more interactive platform to read her work. It contains short stories and novelettes based off the Danarko Multi-Realm as well as other exclusive content. Members have access to certain levels depending on their subscription.

Learn more about the *Sealed Archives* and read exclusive stories here:

www.patreon.com/storibrook

ABOUT THE AUTHOR

Maxina Storibrook grew up traveling all over the world. She loved it so much she couldn't be satisfied by merely traveling to all the unknown places across the Earth; she has to discover new places, write about other worlds, and meet amazing, adventurous people.

Maxina has a bachelor's degree in English and a master's degree in creative writing – all for the love of words. The *Danarko Saga* is her first series, and she takes pride in all the effort she has put into her realms.

In Silver Grove Publications, she hopes to bring beautiful content to people's lives.

Her biggest dream? *To tell stories.*

Explore Maxina's written works and learn more about her: www.maxinastoribrook.com

Get exclusive content on Patreon: www.patreon.com/storibrook

Purchase signed copies, find out more about Silver Grove Publications, and explore other SGP Authors: www.silvergrovepublications.com